Jingle Bells

'*T*is Christmas Eve!
  Dear Santa Claus will bring
    his gifts tonight.
We'll hang our stockings by the fire,
    and wait until it's light.
I wonder what he'll bring for you
    and what he'll bring for me.
Ah! There! It's no use wondering.
    You'll have to wait and see!

—*Anon*

Jingle Bells

Nick Butterworth

ORCHARD BOOKS • NEW YORK

CHRISTMAS TIME.

A happy time, or so it should be. Why, then, on this Christmas Eve, did two small mice look so unhappy?

"It's That Cat," grumbled Lottie to her brother, Jack. "He always spoils things."

Ah, yes. That Cat.

It should have been wonderful for the mice, living in a stable on a farm. There were games to play, places to explore, and usually, plenty to eat.

There was only one problem . . .
That Cat.

The mice had been hiding food for their Christmas dinner, but the cat had discovered their hiding place.

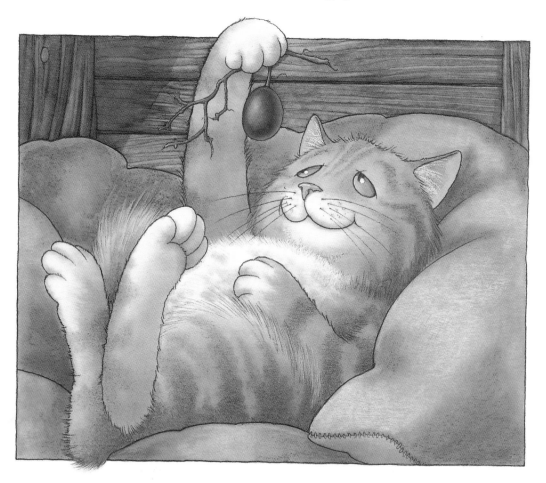

He didn't particularly like cake or cheese or apple. But still, he had eaten every bit and left the mice with nothing. That Cat.

"Cheer up," said Jack. "Look what I've found." It was an old glove. Jack began to chew at it.

"We can't eat that," said Lottie.

Jack went on chewing. Soon he had gnawed off two of the glove's fingers.

"There!" he said. "Christmas stockings! One each. We can hang them up for Santa Claus."

"Brilliant!" said Lottie. "I've never had a Christmas stocking."

That night, as the mice snuggled down to sleep, they wondered what Santa Claus would bring them.

Lottie had written their names on a note that she put next to their Christmas stockings so Santa Claus would know who they were for.

S oon Lottie began to snore, Jack began
to dream, and the air was filled with
the sound of sleigh bells.

CHRISTMAS MORNING.
The day was fresh and bright as Lottie and Jack hurried excitedly to look at their Christmas stockings.

They were empty.

"Nothing," said Jack sadly. "Not even a nut."

Lottie picked up the note that she had written the night before.

"Look at this!" she said. Underneath their names, someone had written:

NOT HERE —
GON AWAY
FOR CRISMUS

"I know who wrote that," said Jack. They both knew.

"It's time we taught That Cat a lesson," said Lottie.

"But what can we do?" said Jack. "He's so big and strong."

"Well," said Lottie, "I think we should go and talk to Ton-Chee."

Ton-Chee was a rat. Actually, his real name was Gavin, but he liked to be called Ton-Chee.

He wore glasses that had no glass in them. And he wore clothes that he had "borrowed" from dolls in the farmhouse attic.

He also "borrowed" furniture from
a doll's house, which he said
made his own place more homey.

Lottie and Jack made their way through the snow toward the barn where Ton-Chee lived. Suddenly Jack spotted something. It was shiny and golden.

"It's a bell!" said Jack.

"It's a sleigh bell," said Lottie. "It must have fallen off Santa Claus's sleigh. It's lovely. Let's take it with us. We'll show it to Ton-Chee."

When the mice reached the barn, they were quite out of breath, but there was still a difficult climb to make.

At last, puffing and panting, they came to a little door at the top of the barn.

B efore Jack could knock, the door
opened.

"Good morning! And a very merry
Christmas to you," said the rat. The mice
smiled and replied nervously. Then they
stepped inside. Ton-Chee shut the door.

It is hard to say exactly what the mice and the rat said to each other. But whatever it was, when the door opened again, all three were smiling.

"Thank you very much," said Lottie and Jack together. Ton-Chee smiled.

"The pleasure is all mine," he said. "Cats can be such a terrible nuisance."

Later, after a Christmas dinner of some "borrowed" fruitcake that Ton-Chee had given to them, the mice could be seen wrapping up a parcel.

Later still, they tried not to be seen as they cautiously carried their parcel toward the farmhouse.

THE DAY AFTER CHRISTMAS.
Mrs. Mackie, the farmer's wife,
swung her feet out of bed and into her
slippers. At the foot of the stairs, the cat
brushed past her legs.

"Hello, Angus," she said. "What's this?"
She picked up a small parcel that
lay on the mat and read the label.

"It's an extra present for you, Angus!" she
said to the cat.

Angus watched as Mrs. Mackie opened
the parcel. What could it be?

"It's a little bell!" said Mrs. Mackie, "on a pretty red ribbon!"

To Angus
with love
X X X

Before he could escape, Mrs. Mackie took a firm hold of Angus and tied the ribbon around his neck. The little bell jingled under his chin.

"There!" she said. "You look lovely!"
Angus twisted his neck uncomfortably,
and the bell jingled again.

He made a face and pawed at the bell.
"Don't you dare," said Mrs. Mackie.
"You keep it on."

It was late afternoon, around teatime.

Lottie and Jack were having great fun in the snow. Suddenly they stopped and listened. They could hear the jingling of a little bell.

"Quick! Someone's coming," whispered Lottie.

The mice ran to hide in the stable.

As they peered out, they saw a very cross-looking Angus go stalking past. He looked from side to side and shook his head. The little bell jingled merrily.

"Hmmph!" grunted Angus, and he stumped off, jingling as he went.

The mice burst into a fit of giggles, and Lottie began to sing: *"Jingle bells, jingle bells, jingle all the way. . . . Now Angus can't sneak up on us when we go out to play!"*

They laughed and laughed.

"It may not have been a very merry Christmas," said Jack, "but it does look like a Happy New Year!"

Orchard Books
95 Madison Avenue
New York, NY 10016

Manufactured in China

1 3 5 7 9 10 8 6 4 2

The text of this book is set in 18 point ITC Garamond Light BT.
The illustrations are watercolor.

Library of Congress Cataloging-in-Publication Data
Butterworth, Nick.
Jingle bells / Nick Butterworth.
p. cm.
Summary: After Angus the cat spoils their Christmas, two mice
named Lottie and Jack contrive a plan to keep out of Angus's way.
ISBN 0-531-30124-9 (alk. paper)
[1. Mice—Fiction. 2. Cats—Fiction. 3. Christmas—Fiction.] I. Title.
PZ7.B98225Ji 1998 [E]—dc21 98-15436

NICK BUTTERWORTH is a designer,
artist, and author with more than fifty
books to his credit. He lives in Suffolk,
England with his wife, Annette, and
their two children, Ben and Amanda.